Arthur Geisert

THE ARK

Houghton Mifflin Company
Boston   1988

For my parents, Leonard and Doris Geisert

Library of Congress Cataloging-in-Publication Data

Geisert, Arthur.
  The ark / Arthur Geisert.
    p. cm.
    Summary: Retells the familiar Bible story, noting how life went on
inside the ark.
    ISBN 0-395-43078-X
    1. Noah's ark — Juvenile literature. [1. Noah's ark. 2. Bible
stories — O. T.] I. Title.
BS658.G37   1988   88-15889
222'.1109505 — dc19   CIP
                          AC

Printed in the United States of America

NS 10 9 8 7 6 5 4 3 2 1

THE ARK

The Lord saw that the wickedness of man was great in the earth, and
it grieved him to his heart. So the Lord said, "I will blot out man
whom I have created from the face of the ground, man and beast and
creeping things and birds of the air, for I am sorry that I have
made them."
But Noah found favor in the eyes of the Lord.

From the book of Genesis

Noah and his sons were commanded to build an ark.

It would be large enough to carry Noah, his wife, his three sons and their wives,

and one male and one female of every creature from the earth.

One evening, the animals began their journey to the ark.

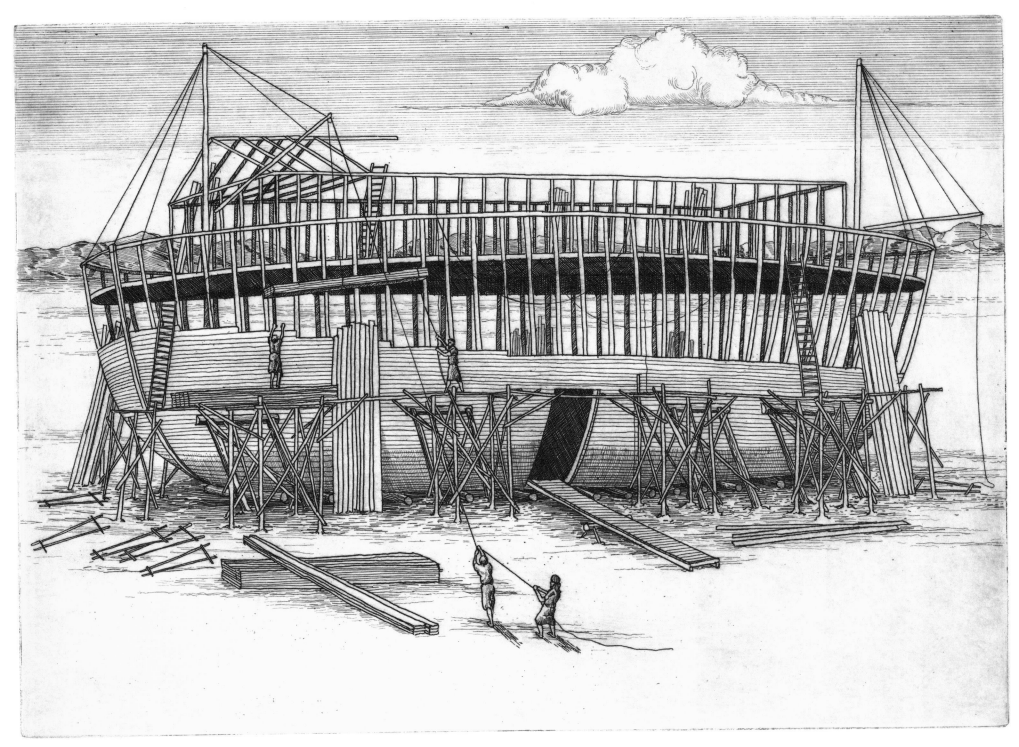

The next day a cloud appeared in the sky.

And the animals began to arrive.

Another cloud soon appeared.

More animals arrived.

The outside of the ark was finished as many more clouds appeared.

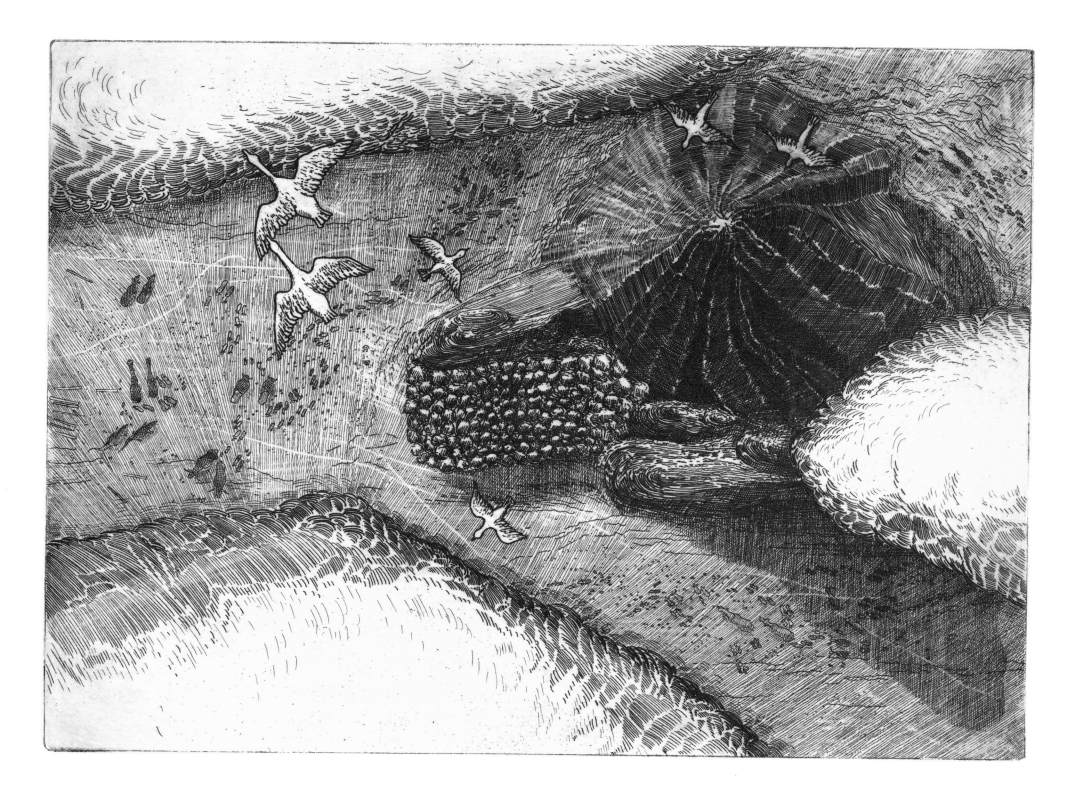

The wives tended the animals.

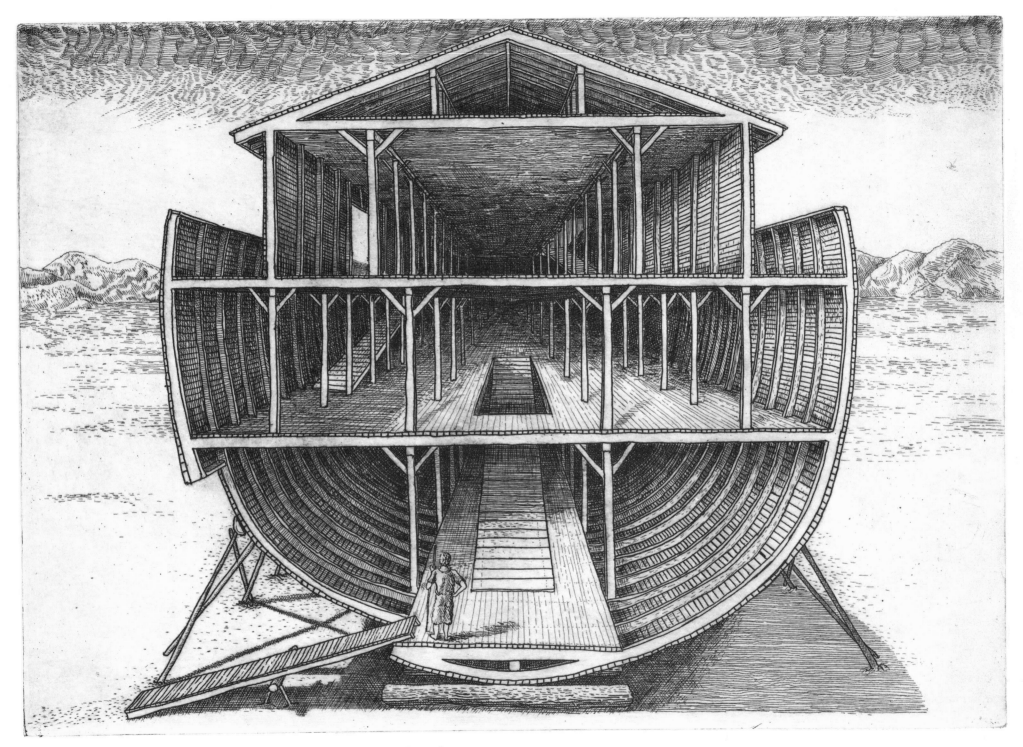

Noah and his sons worked quickly to finish the ark.

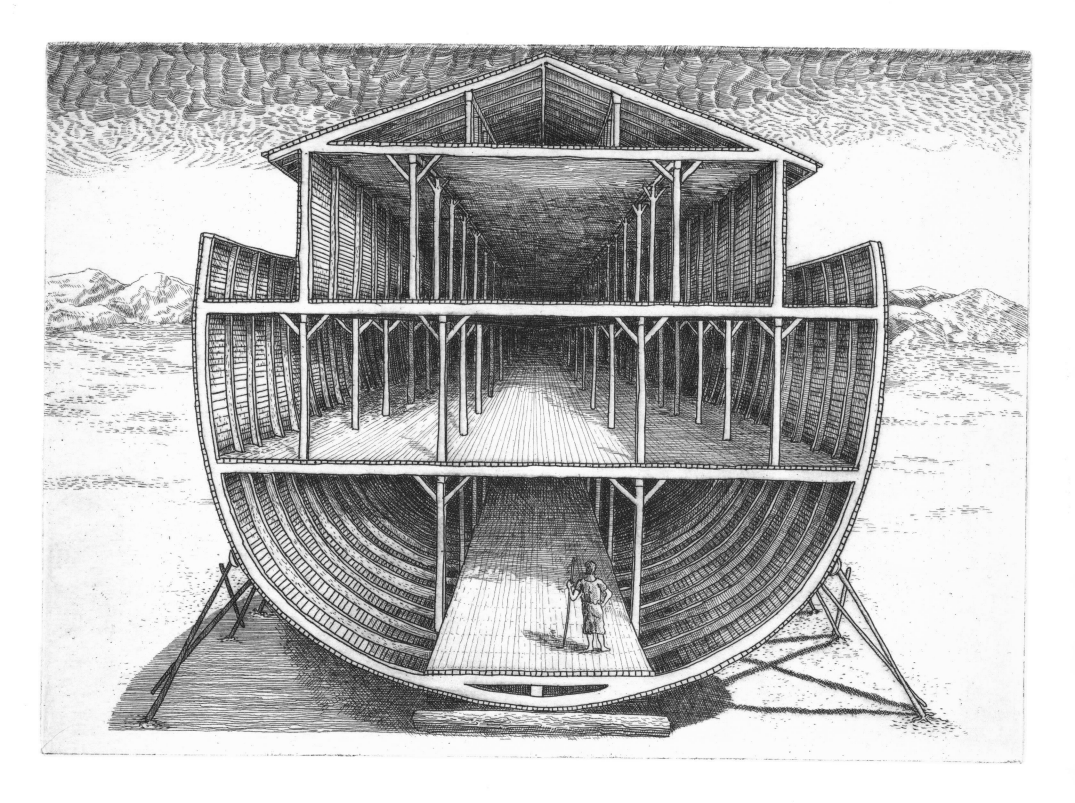

Rain started to fall.

It was time to board the ark.

After the animals had boarded, the door was sealed.

Noah was last to board.

The heavens opened and the rain poured down.

It rained for many days and many nights.

Inside the ark it was warm, dry, and very crowded.

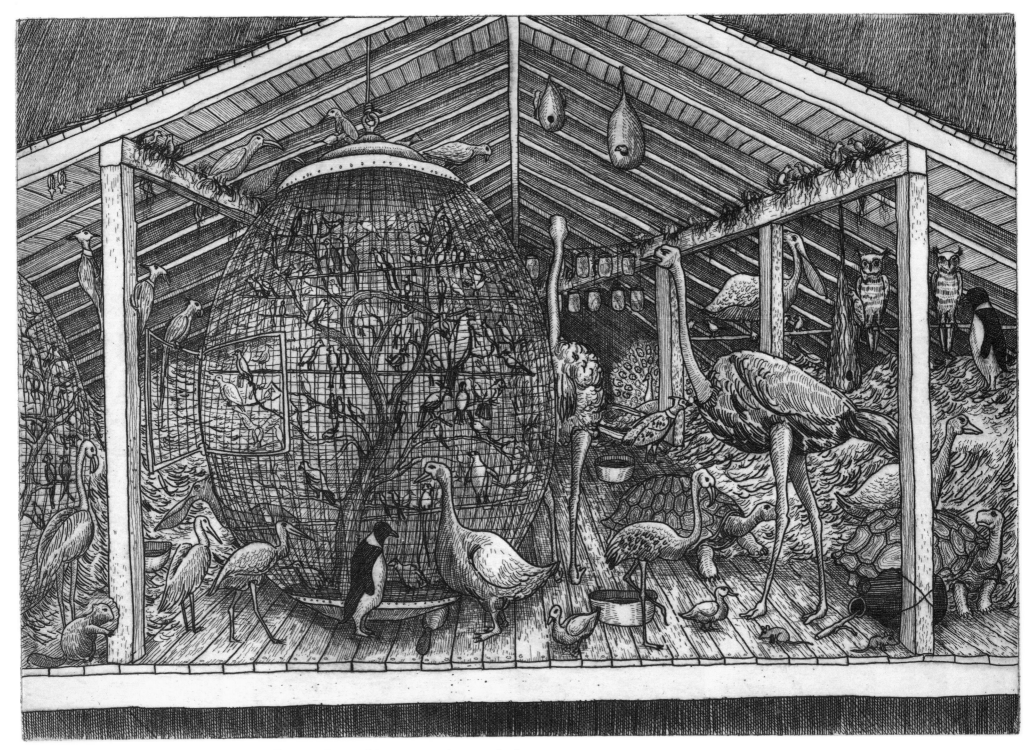

Noah put the birds, small animals, and insects on the top deck.

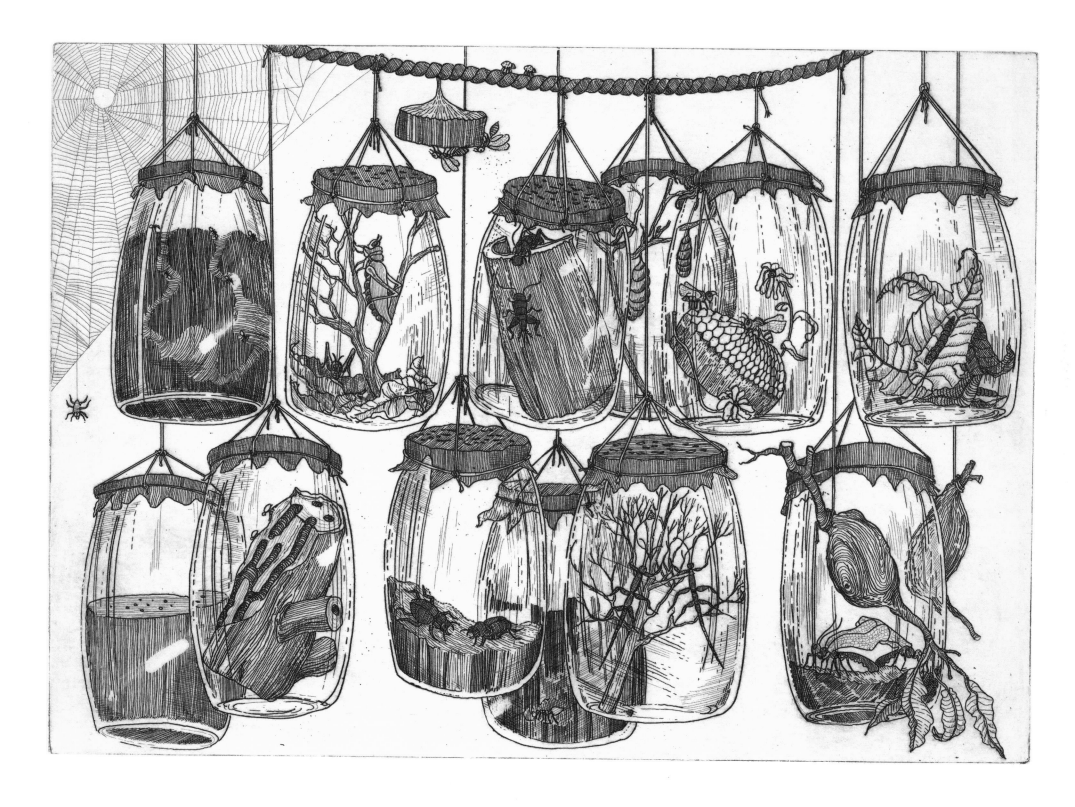

Watering and feeding the animals was a never-ending job.

Everyone had to work to keep the ark clean.

Fish and sea creatures swam outside close to the hull.

The largest animals were kept on the lower deck.

The animals learned to live together in almost perfect harmony.

The family found time to rest only at dinner.

They went to bed each night exhausted from the day's hard work.

The rains fell until the whole world was covered by water.

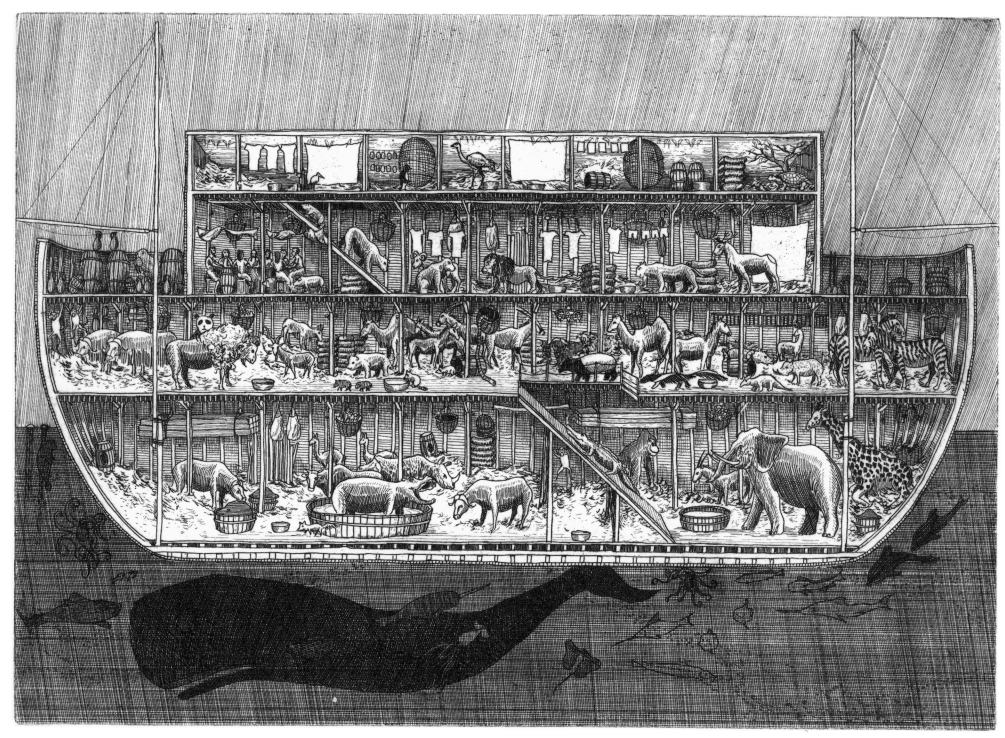

There was a place for everything inside the ark. But everything did not always stay in its place.

Finally, the rain stopped.

The sun shone, and all on the ark welcomed the light.

Then Noah sent out a dove.

When the dove returned with an olive branch, Noah knew that life on the earth could begin again.

The waters receded and the ark finally came to rest.

The door was unsealed and the animals went forth.

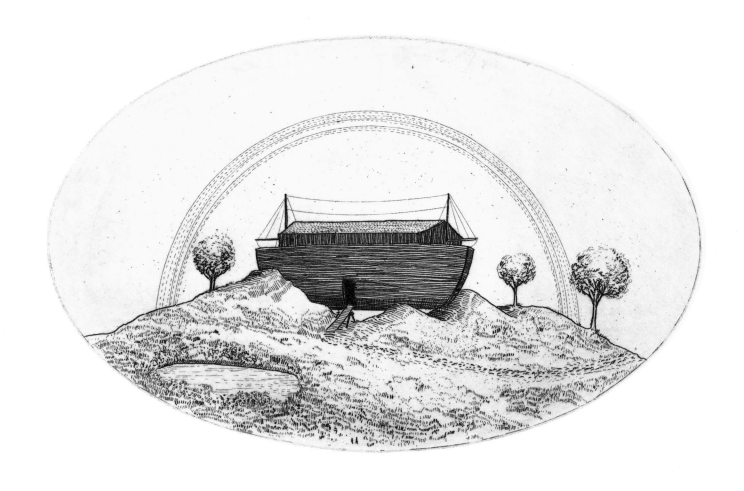

The Lord then sent a rainbow as a sign that there would never again be a flood to destroy the creatures of the earth.